To moms and dads,
especially my own

Farrar Straus Giroux Books for Young Readers
175 Fifth Avenue, New York 10010

Copyright © 2015 by James Kwan
All rights reserved
Color separations by Embassy Graphics
Printed in China by Macmillan Production (Asia) Ltd.,
Kowloon Bay, Hong Kong (Supplier code 10)
Designed by Roberta Pressel
First edition, 2015
10 9 8 7 6 5 4 3 2 1

mackids.com

Library of Congress Cataloging-in-Publication Data
Kwan, James, author, illustrator.
    Dear Yeti / James Kwan. — First edition.
        pages cm
    Summary: Told through a series of notes, two boys go on a hike hoping to find Yeti but run into
    trouble along the way.
    ISBN 978-0-374-30045-6 (hardcover)
    [1. Yeti—Fiction.   2. Hiking—Fiction.   3. Letters—Fiction.   4. Humorous stories.]   I. Title.

PZ7.1.K92De 2015
[E]—dc23
                                                                                                2015002575

Farrar Straus Giroux Books for Young Readers may be purchased for business or promotional use.
For information on bulk purchases please contact Macmillan Corporate and Premium Sales Department
at (800) 221-7945 x5442 or by email at specialmarkets@macmillan.com.

James Kwan

DEAR YETI

WITHDRAWN

Farrar Straus Giroux • New York

Dear Yeti,
    We're searching for you.
        Sincerely,
        Hikers

Dear Yeti,
    We're calling your name. You
are one hard beast to find! We
are wild, but friendly, men. You
shouldn't be shy.

                    Hikers

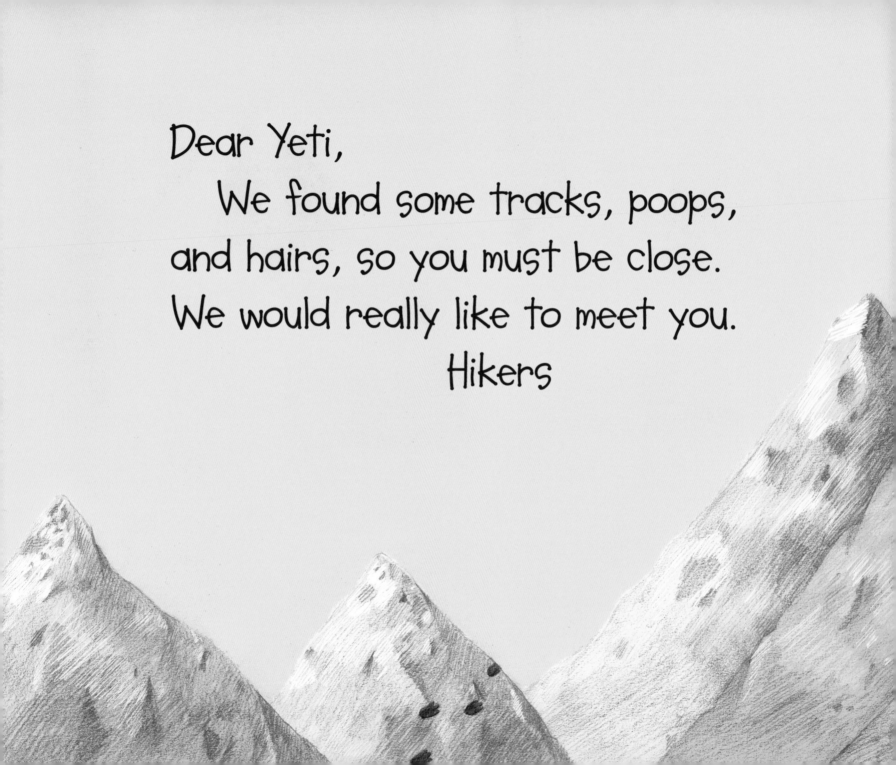

Dear Yeti,
    We found some tracks, poops,
and hairs, so you must be close.
We would really like to meet you.
                    Hikers

Dear Yeti,
   Morale is still high,
but food supplies are low.
      Hikers

Dear Yeti,
    We found some berries.
They were delicious.
Were they from you?
        Hikers

Dear Yeti,
   The forest is getting darker.
The wind is howling loudly.

Dear Yeti,
    We found a snow cave
to hide out from the storm.
    Are you safe and warm,
        too?
                Hikers

"Can you hear those spooky sounds?"

"I hope it's not a grizzly bear."

"Please don't eat my new friends."

It's late and we have to get back home.
Can you help us find our way?"

"Goodbye."

Dear Hikers,
See you soon.

Love,
Yeti